Grapefully yours,

Kimberly DesJardins :)

For my beloved Bruce bunch – Keith, Madeleine, and Mason.
– KD –

To Heidi for letting me be my quirky, green, self.
– BH –

Gabby

the GREEN GRAPE ©

Written by Kimberly DesJardine & Illustrated by Bill Hart

Published by The Bunch, LLC, Novato CA.
Text and illustrations Copyright © 2014 by Kimberly DesJardine and Bill Hart. All rights reserved.

Visit www.gabbythegreengrape.com
Printed in Canada
Library of Congress Control Number: 2014911156
ISBN 978-0-578-14447-4

This is...

...Gabby!

She lived with her family, the Grapes.

Mama Grape

Papa Grape

Gabby Grape

Gavin Grape

and Squirt.

Grape-Ma and Grape-Pa lived with them, too.

Together they were quite a bunch!

Gabby liked to hang with her family
on a vineyard in the country.

As the summer approached and the hot sun shone down,
the grapes slowly all began to turn purple.

All except for Gabby...

Gabby liked being green.

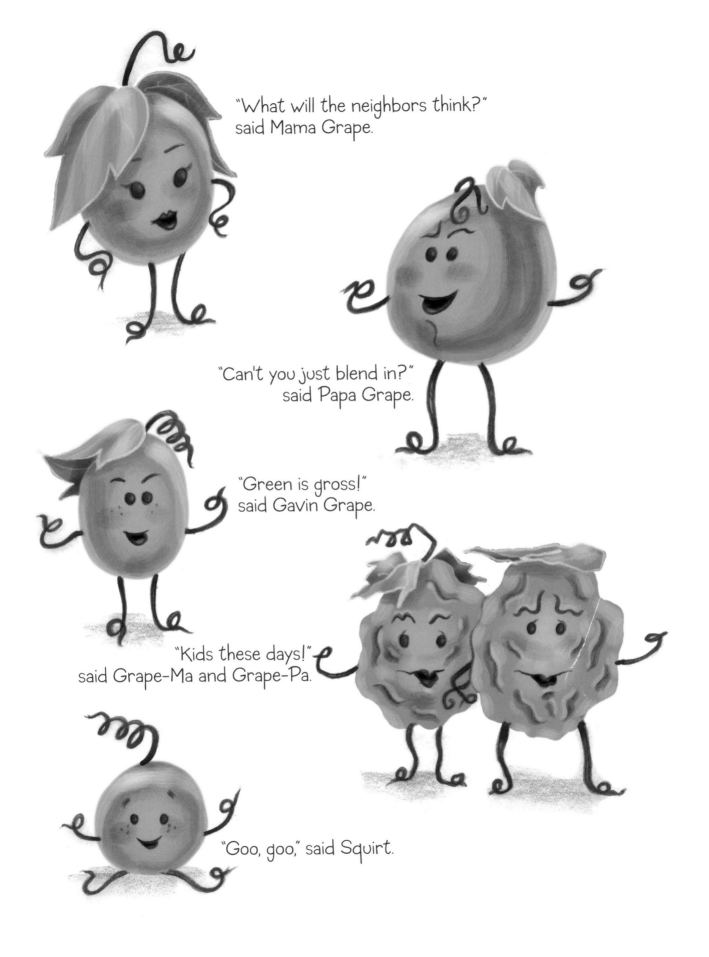

"What will the neighbors think?"
said Mama Grape.

"Can't you just blend in?"
said Papa Grape.

"Green is gross!"
said Gavin Grape.

"Kids these days!"
said Grape-Ma and Grape-Pa.

"Goo, goo," said Squirt.

Gabby didn't care. "Green is keen!"

"Green is gorgeous!"

"Green is groovy," she said.

But at school, the kids also questioned her.

"Green?!" said Gidget.
"Grow up," said Gordon.

"Get with it," said Grace.
"Good grief," sighed her teacher Mrs. Givens.

Gabby didn't care, she liked being different.

But, no one seemed to understand.

So, she tried to explain…

"Green is the new purple!"

"Be green,
keep your vineyard clean!"

...but nothing seemed to help.

With each passing day,
the grapes got grapier,

... but Gabby got greener.

One September day,
a worker carrying a basket visited the vineyard.

Without warning, he began picking

the warm, purple bunches of grapes.

He came upon the Grape family,
peered closely at them and muttered,
"Not ripe, still green." The man moved on.

Soon the Grape family was the only bunch left in the vineyard.

"We are grateful you're green," said Mama Grape.

"Green saved our skins!" said Papa Grape.

"Green's the scene!" said Gavin Grape.

"Goodness green-ness," said Grape-Ma and Grape-Pa.

"Goo, goo," said Squirt.

One year later...

...a worker carrying a basket visited the same vineyard.

There was nothing to gather though,
because the grapes grew green!

Gabby grinned with glee!

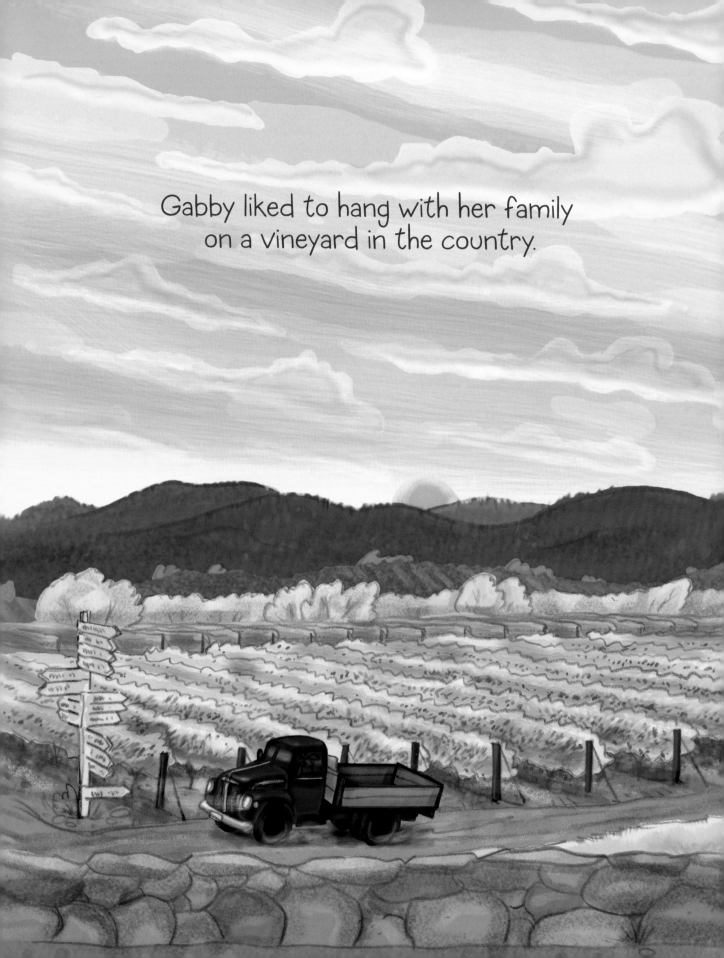

Gabby liked to hang with her family
on a vineyard in the country.